Thoughts Sugg

Mr. Froude's "Progress"

Charles Dudley Warner

Alpha Editions

This edition published in 2023

ISBN : 9789357945684

Design and Setting By
Alpha Editions
www.alphaedis.com
Email - info@alphaedis.com

Contents

THOUGHTS SUGGESTED BY MR. FROUDE'S "PROGRESS"

BY CHARLES DUDLEY WARNER

To revisit this earth, some ages after their departure from it, is a common wish among men. We frequently hear men say that they would give so many months or years of their lives in exchange for a less number on the globe one or two or three centuries from now. Merely to see the world from some remote sphere, like the distant spectator of a play which passes in dumb show, would not suffice. They would like to be of the world again, and enter into its feelings, passions, hopes; to feel the sweep of its current, and so to comprehend what it has become.

I suppose that we all who are thoroughly interested in this world have this desire. There are some select souls who sit apart in calm endurance, waiting to be translated out of a world they are almost tired of patronizing, to whom the whole thing seems, doubtless, like a cheap performance. They sit on the fence of criticism, and cannot for the life of them see what the vulgar crowd make such a toil and sweat about. The prizes are the same dreary, old, fading bay wreaths. As for the soldiers marching past, their uniforms are torn, their hats are shocking, their shoes are dusty, they do not appear (to a man sitting on the fence) to march with any kind of spirit, their flags are old and tattered, the drums they beat are barbarous; and, besides, it is not probable that they are going anywhere; they will merely come round again, the same people, like the marching chorus in the "Beggar's Opera." Such critics, of course, would not care to see the vulgar show over again; it is enough for them to put on record their protest against it in the weekly "Judgment Days" which they edit, and by-and-by withdraw out of their private boxes, with pity for a world in the creation of which they were not consulted.

The desire to revisit this earth is, I think, based upon a belief, well-nigh universal, that the world is to make some progress, and that it will be more interesting in the future than it is now. I believe that the human mind, whenever it is developed enough to comprehend its own action, rests, and has always rested, in this expectation. I do not know any period of time in which the civilized mind has not had expectation of something better for the race in the future. This expectation is sometimes stronger than it is at others; and, again, there are always those who say that the Golden Age is behind them. It is always behind or before us; the poor present alone has no friends; the present, in the minds of many, is only the car that is carrying us away from an age of virtue and of happiness, or that is perhaps bearing us on to a time of ease and comfort and security.

Perhaps it is worth while, in view of certain recent discussions, and especially of some free criticisms of this country, to consider whether there is any intention of progress in this world, and whether that intention is discoverable in the age in which we live.

If it is an old question, it is not a settled one; the practical disbelief in any such progress is widely entertained. Not long ago Mr. James Anthony Froude published an essay on Progress, in which he examined some of the evidences upon which we rely to prove that we live in an "era of progress." It is a melancholy essay, for its tone is that of profound skepticism as to certain influences and means of progress upon which we in this country most rely. With the illustrative arguments of Mr. Froude's essay I do not purpose specially to meddle; I recall it to the attention of the reader as a representative type of skepticism regarding progress which is somewhat common among intellectual men, and is not confined to England. It is not exactly an acceptance of Rousseau's notion that civilization is a mistake, and that it would be better for us all to return to a state of nature—though in John Ruskin's case it nearly amounts to this; but it is a hostility in its last analysis to what we understand by the education of the people, and to the government of the people by themselves. If Mr. Froude's essay is anything but an exhibition of the scholarly weapons of criticism, it is the expression of a profound disbelief in the intellectual education of the masses of the people. Mr. Ruskin goes further. He makes his open proclamation against any emancipation from hand-toil. Steam is the devil himself let loose from the pit, and all labor-saving machinery is his own invention. Mr. Ruskin is the bull that stands upon the track and threatens with annihilation the on-coming locomotive; and I think that any spectator who sees his menacing attitude and hears his roaring cannot but have fears for the locomotive.

There are two sorts of infidelity concerning humanity, and I do not know which is the more withering in its effects. One is that which regards this world as only a waste and a desert, across the sands of which we are merely fugitives, fleeing from the wrath to come. The other is that doubt of any divine intention in development, in history, which we call progress from age to age.

In the eyes of this latter infidelity history is not a procession or a progression, but only a series of disconnected pictures, each little era rounded with its own growth, fruitage, and decay, a series of incidents or experiments, without even the string of a far-reaching purpose to connect them. There is no intention of progress in it all. The race is barbarous, and then it changes to civilized; in the one case the strong rob the weak by brute force; in the other the crafty rob the unwary by finesse. The latter is a more agreeable state of things; but it comes to about the same. The robber used to knock us down and take away our sheepskins; he now administers chloroform and relieves us of our watches. It is a gentlemanly proceeding, and scientific, and we call it civilization. Meantime human nature remains the same, and the whole thing is a weary round that has no advance in it.

If this is true the succession of men and of races is no better than a vegetable succession; and Mr. Froude is quite right in doubting if education of the brain will do the English agricultural laborer any good; and Mr. Ruskin ought to be aided in his crusade against machinery, which turns the world upside down. The best that can be done with a man is the best that can be done with a plant-set him out in some favorable locality, or leave him where he happened to strike root, and there let him grow and mature in measure and quiet—especially quiet—as he may in God's sun and rain. If he happens to be a cabbage, in Heaven's name don't try to make a rose of him, and do not disturb the vegetable maturing of his head by grafting ideas upon his stock.

The most serious difficulty in the way of those who maintain that there is an intention of progress in this world from century to century, from age to age—a discernible growth, a universal development—is the fact that all nations do not make progress at the same time or in the same ratio; that nations reach a certain development, and then fall away and even retrograde; that while one may be advancing into high civilization, another is lapsing into deeper barbarism, and that nations appear to have a limit of growth. If there were a law of progress, an intention of it in all the world, ought not all peoples and tribes to advance pari passu, or at least ought there not to be discernible a general movement, historical and contemporary? There is no such general movement which can be computed, the law of which can be discovered—therefore it does not exist. In a kind of despair, we are apt to run over in our minds empires and pre-eminent civilizations that have existed, and then to doubt whether life in this world is intended to be anything more than a series of experiments. There is the German nation of our day, the most aggressive in various fields of intellectual activity, a Hercules of scholarship, the most thoroughly trained and powerful—though its civilization marches to the noise of the hateful and barbarous drum. In what points is it better than the Greek nation of the age of its superlative artists, philosophers, poets—the age of the most joyous, elastic human souls in the most perfect human bodies?

Again, it is perhaps a fanciful notion that the Atlantis of Plato was the northern part of the South American continent, projecting out towards Africa, and that the Antilles are the peaks and headlands of its sunken bulk. But there are evidences enough that the shores of the Gulf of Mexico and the Caribbean Sea were within historic periods the seat of a very considerable civilization—the seat of cities, of commerce, of trade, of palaces and pleasure—gardens—faint images, perhaps, of the luxurious civilization of Baia! and Pozzuoli and Capri in the most profligate period of the Roman empire. It is not more difficult to believe that there was a great material development here than to believe it of the African shore of the Mediterranean. Not to multiply instances that will occur to all, we see as many retrograde as advance movements, and we see, also, that while one spot of the earth at one time seems to be the chosen theatre of progress, other portions of the globe are absolutely dead and without the least leaven of advancing life, and we cannot understand how this can be if there is any such thing as an all-pervading and animating intention or law of progress. And then we are reminded that the individual human mind long ago attained its height of power and capacity. It is enough to recall the names of Moses, Buddha, Confucius, Socrates, Paul, Homer, David.

No doubt it has seemed to other periods and other nations, as it now does to the present civilized races, that they were the chosen times and peoples of an extraordinary and limitless development. It must have seemed so to the Jews who overran Palestine and set their shining cities on all the hills of heathendom. It must have seemed so to the Babylonish conquerors who swept over Palestine in turn, on their way to greater conquests in Egypt. It must have seemed so to Greece when the Acropolis was to the outlying world what the imperial calla is to the marsh in which it lifts its superb flower. It must have seemed so to Rome when its solid roads of stone ran to all parts of a tributary world—the highways of the legions, her ministers, and of the wealth that poured into her treasury. It must have seemed so to followers of Mahomet, when the crescent knew no pause in its march up the Arabian peninsula to the Bosporus, to India, along the Mediterranean shores to Spain, where in the eighth century it flowered into a culture, a learning, a refinement in art and manners, to which the Christian world of that day was a stranger. It must have seemed so in the awakening of the sixteenth century, when Europe, Spain leading, began that great movement of discovery and aggrandizement which has, in the end, been profitable only to a portion of the adventurers. And what shall we say of a nation as old, if not older than any of these we have mentioned, slowly building up meantime a civilization and perfecting a system of government and a social economy which should outlast them all, and remain to our day almost the sole monument of permanence and stability in a shifting world?

How many times has the face of Europe been changed—and parts of Africa, and Asia Minor too, for that matter—by conquests and crusades, and the rise and fall of civilizations as well as dynasties? while China has endured, almost undisturbed, under a system of law, administration, morality, as old as the Pyramids probably—existed a coherent nation, highly developed in certain essentials, meeting and mastering, so far as we can see, the great problem of an over-populated territory, living in a good degree of peace and social order, of respect for age and law, and making a continuous history, the mere record of which is printed in a thousand bulky volumes. Yet we speak of the Chinese empire as an instance of arrested growth, for which there is no salvation, except it shall catch the spirit of progress abroad in the world. What is this progress, and where does it come from?

Think for a moment of this significant situation. For thousands of years, empires, systems of society, systems of civilization—Egyptian, Jewish, Greek, Roman, Moslem, Feudal—have flourished and fallen, grown to a certain height and passed away; great organized fabrics have gone down, and, if there has been any progress, it has been as often defeated as renewed. And here is an empire, apart from this scene of alternate success and disaster, which has existed in a certain continuity and stability, and yet, now that it is uncovered and stands face to face with the rest of the world, it finds that it has little to teach us, and almost everything to learn from us. The old empire sends its students to learn of us, the newest child of civilization; and through us they learn all the great past, its literature, law, science, out of which we sprang. It appears, then, that progress has, after all, been with the shifting world, that has been all this time going to pieces, rather than with the world that has been permanent and unshaken.

When we speak of progress we may mean two things. We may mean a lifting of the races as a whole by reason of more power over the material world, by reason of what we call the conquest of nature and a practical use of its forces; or we may mean a higher development of the individual man, so that he shall be better and happier. If from age to age it is discoverable that the earth is better adapted to man as a dwelling-place, and he is on the whole fitted to get more out of it for his own growth, is not that progress, and is it not evidence of an intention of progress?

Now, it is sometimes said that Providence, in the economy of this world, cares nothing for the individual, but works out its ideas and purposes through the races, and in certain periods, slowly bringing in, by great agencies and by processes destructive to individuals and to millions of helpless human beings, truths and principles; so laying stepping-stones onward to a great consummation. I do not care to dwell upon this thought, but let us see if we can find any evidence in history of the presence in this world of an intention of progress.

It is common to say that, if the world makes progress at all, it is by its great men, and when anything important for the race is to be done, a great man is raised up to do it. Yet another way to look at it is, that the doing of something at the appointed time makes the man who does it great, or at least celebrated. The man often appears to be only a favored instrument of communication. As we glance back we recognize the truth that, at this and that period, the time had come for certain discoveries. Intelligence seemed pressing in from the invisible. Many minds were on the alert to apprehend it. We believe, for instance, that if Gutenberg had not invented movable types, somebody else would have given them to the world about that time. Ideas, at certain times, throng for admission into the world; and we are all familiar with the fact that the same important idea (never before revealed in all the ages) occurs to separate and widely distinct minds at about the same time. The invention of the electric telegraph seemed to burst upon the world simultaneously from many quarters—not perfect, perhaps, but the time for the idea had come—and happy was it for the man who entertained it. We have agreed to call Columbus the discoverer of America, but I suppose there is no doubt that America had been visited by European, and probably Asiatic, people ages before Columbus; that four or five centuries before him people from northern Europe had settlements here; he was fortunate, however, in "discovering" it in the fullness of time, when the world, in its progress, was ready for it. If the Greeks had had gunpowder, electro-magnetism, the printing press, history would need to be rewritten. Why the inquisitive Greek mind did not find out these things is a mystery upon any other theory than the one we are considering.

And it is as mysterious that China, having gunpowder and the art of printing, is not today like Germany.

There seems to me to be a progress, or an intention of progress, in the world, independent of individual men. Things get on by all sorts of instruments, and sometimes by very poor ones. There are times when new thoughts or applications of known principles seem to throng from the invisible for expression through human media, and there is hardly ever an important invention set free in the world that men do not appear to be ready cordially to receive it. Often we should be justified in saying that there was a widespread expectation of it. Almost all the great inventions and the ingenious application of principles have many claimants for the honor of priority.

On any other theory than this, that there is present in the world an intention of progress which outlasts individuals, and even races, I cannot account for the fact that, while civilizations decay and pass away, and human systems go to pieces, ideas remain and accumulate. We, the latest age, are the inheritors of all the foregoing ages. I do not believe that anything of importance has been lost to the world. The Jewish civilization was torn up root and branch, but whatever was valuable in the Jewish polity is ours now. We may say the same of the civilizations of Athens and of Rome; though the entire organization of the ancient world, to use Mr. Froude's figure, collapsed into a heap of incoherent sand, the ideas remained, and Greek art and Roman law are part of the world's solid possessions.

Even those who question the value to the individual of what we call progress, admit, I suppose, the increase of knowledge in the world from age to age, and not only its increase, but its diffusion. The intelligent schoolboy today knows more than the ancient sages knew—more about the visible heavens, more of the secrets of the earth, more of the human body. The rudiments of his education, the common experiences of his everyday life, were, at the best, the guesses and speculations of a remote age. There is certainly an accumulation of facts, ideas, knowledge. Whether this makes men better, wiser, happier, is indeed disputed.

In order to maintain the notion of a general and intended progress, it is not necessary to show that no preceding age has excelled ours in some special, development. Phidias has had no rival in sculpture, we may admit. It is possible that glass was once made as flexible as leather, and that copper could be hardened like steel. But I do not take much stock in the "lost arts," the wondering theme of the lyceums. The knowledge of the natural world, and of materials, was never, I believe, so extensive and exact as it is today. It is possible that there are tricks of chemistry, ingenious processes, secrets of color, of which we are ignorant; but I do not believe there was ever an ancient alchemist who could not be taught something in a modern laboratory. The vast engineering works of the ancient Egyptians, the remains of their temples and pyramids, excite our wonder; but I have no doubt that President Grant, if he becomes the tyrant they say he is becoming, and commands the labor of forty millions of slaves—a large proportion of them office —holders—could build a Karnak, or erect a string of pyramids across New Jersey.

Mr. Froude runs lightly over a list of subjects upon which the believer in progress relies for his belief, and then says of them that the world calls this progress—he calls it only change. I suppose he means by this two things: that these great movements of our modern life are not any evidence of a permanent advance, and that our whole structure may tumble into a heap of incoherent sand, as systems of society have done before; and, again, that it is questionable if, in what we call a stride in civilization, the individual citizen is becoming any purer or more just, or if his intelligence is directed towards learning and doing what is right, or only to the means of more extended pleasures.

It is, perhaps, idle to speculate upon the first of these points—the permanence of our advance, if it is an advance. But we may be encouraged by one thing that distinguishes this period—say from the middle of the eighteenth century—from any that has preceded it. I mean the introduction of machinery, applied to the multiplication of man's power in a hundred directions—to manufacturing, to locomotion, to the diffusion of thought and of knowledge. I need not dwell upon this familiar topic. Since this period began there has been, so far as I know, no retrograde movement anywhere, but, besides the material, an intellectual and spiritual kindling the world over, for which history has no sort of parallel. Truth is always the same, and will make its way, but this subject might be illustrated by a study of the relation of Christianity and of the brotherhood of men to machinery. The theme would demand an essay by itself. I leave it with the one remark, that this great change now being wrought in the world by the multiplicity of machinery is not more a material than it is an intellectual one, and that we have no instance in history of a catastrophe widespread enough and adequate to sweep away its results. That is to say, none of the catastrophes, not even the corruptions, which brought to ruin the ancient civilizations, would work anything like the same disaster in an age which has the use of machinery that this age has.

For instance: Gibbon selects the period between the accession of Trajan and the death of Marcus Aurelius as the time in which the human race enjoyed more general happiness than they had ever known before, or had since known. Yet, says Mr. Froude, in the midst of this prosperity the heart of the empire was dying out of it; luxury and selfishness were eating away the principle that held society together, and the ancient world was on the point of collapsing into a heap of incoherent sand. Now, it is impossible to conceive that the catastrophe which did happen to that civilization could have happened if the world had then possessed the steam-engine, the printing-press, and the electric telegraph. The Roman power might have gone down, and the face of the world been recast; but such universal chaos and such a relapse for the individual people would seem impossible.

If we turn from these general considerations to the evidences that this is an "era of progress" in the condition of individual men, we are met by more specific denials. Granted, it is said, all your facilities for travel and communication, for cheap and easy manufacture, for the distribution of cheap literature and news, your cheap education, better homes, and all the comforts and luxuries of your machine civilization, is the average man, the agriculturist, the machinist, the laborer any better for it all? Are there more purity, more honest, fair dealing, genuine work, fear and honor of God? Are the proceeds of labor more evenly distributed? These, it is said, are the criteria of progress; all else is misleading.

Now, it is true that the ultimate end of any system of government or civilization should be the improvement of the individual man. And yet this truth, as Mr. Froude puts it, is only a half-truth, so that this single test of any system may not do for a given time and a limited area. Other and wider considerations come in. Disturbances, which for a while unsettle society and do not bring good results to individuals, may, nevertheless, be necessary, and may be a sign of progress. Take the favorite illustration of Mr. Froude and Mr. Ruskin—the condition of the agricultural laborer of England. If I understand them, the civilization of the last century has not helped his position as a man. If I understand them, he was a better man, in a better condition of earthly happiness, and with a better chance of heaven, fifty years ago than now, before the "era of progress" found him out. (It ought to be noticed here, that the report of the Parliamentary Commission on the condition of the English agricultural laborer does not sustain Mr. Froude's assumptions. On the contrary, the report shows that his condition is in almost all respects vastly better than it was fifty years ago.) Mr. Ruskin would remove the steam-engine and all its devilish works from his vicinity; he would abolish factories, speedy travel by rail, new-fangled instruments of agriculture, our patent education, and remit him to his ancient condition— tied for life to a bit of ground, which should supply all his simple wants; his wife should weave the clothes for the family; his children should learn nothing but the catechism and to speak the truth; he should take his religion without question from the hearty, fox-hunting parson, and live and die undisturbed by ideas. Now, it seems to me that if Mr. Ruskin could realize in some isolated nation this idea of a pastoral, simple existence, under a paternal government, he would have in time an ignorant, stupid, brutal community in a great deal worse case than the agricultural laborers of England are at present. Three-fourths of the crime in the kingdom of Bavaria is committed in the Ultramontane region of the Tyrol, where the conditions of popular education are about those that Mr. Ruskin seems to regret as swept away by the present movement in England—a stagnant state of things, in which any wind of heaven would be a blessing, even if it were a tornado. Education of the modern sort unsettles the peasant, renders him unfit for labor, and gives us a half-educated idler in place of a conscientious workman. The disuse of the apprentice system is not made good by the present system of education, because no one learns a trade well, and the consequence is poor work, and a sham civilization generally. There is some truth in these complaints. But the way out is not backward, but forward. The fault is not with education, though it may be with the kind of education. The education must go forward; the man must not be half but wholly educated. It is only half-knowledge like half-training in a trade that is dangerous.

But what I wish to say is, that notwithstanding certain unfavorable things in the condition of the English laborer and mechanic, his chance is better in the main than it was fifty years ago. The world is a better world for him. He has the opportunity to be more of a man. His world is wider, and it is all open to him to go where he will. Mr. Ruskin may not so easily find his ideal, contented peasant, but the man himself begins to apprehend that this is a world of ideas as well as of food and clothes, and I think, if he were consulted, he would have no desire to return to the condition of his ancestors. In fact, the most hopeful symptom in the condition of the English peasant is his discontent. For, as skepticism is in one sense the handmaid of truth, discontent is the mother of progress. The man is comparatively of little use in the world who is contented.

There is another thought pertinent here. It is this: that no man, however humble, can live a full life if he lives to himself alone. He is more of a man, he lives in a higher plane of thought and of enjoyment, the more his communications are extended with his fellows and the wider his sympathies are. I count it a great thing for the English peasant, a solid addition to his life, that he is every day being put into more intimate relations with every other man on the globe.

I know it is said that these are only vague and sentimental notions of progress—notions of a "salvation by machinery." Let us pass to something that may be less vague, even if it be more sentimental. For a hundred years we have reckoned it progress, that the people were taking part in government. We have had a good deal of faith in the proposition put forth at Philadelphia a century ago, that men are, in effect, equal in political rights. Out of this simple proposition springs logically the extension of suffrage, and a universal education, in order that this important function of a government by the people may be exercised intelligently.

Now we are told by the most accomplished English essayists that this is a mistake, that it is change, but no progress. Indeed, there are philosophers in America who think so. At least I infer so from the fact that Mr. Froude fathers one of his definitions of our condition upon an American. When a block of printer's type is by accident broken up and disintegrated, it falls into what is called "pi." The "pi," a mere chaos, is afterwards sorted and distributed, preparatory to being built up into fresh combinations. "A distinguished American friend," says Mr. Froude, "describes Democracy as making pi." It is so witty a sarcasm that I almost think Mr. Froude manufactured it himself. Well, we have been making this "pi" for a hundred years; it seems to be a national dish in considerable favor with the rest of the world—even such ancient nations as China and Japan want a piece of it.

Now, of course, no form of human government is perfect, or anything like it, but I should be willing to submit the question to an English traveler even, whether, on the whole, the people of the United States do not have as fair a chance in life and feel as little the oppression of government as any other in the world; whether anywhere the burdens are more lifted off men's shoulders.

This infidelity to popular government and unbelief in any good results to come from it are not, unfortunately, confined to the English essayists. I am not sure but the notion is growing in what is called the intellectual class, that it is a mistake to intrust the government to the ignorant many, and that it can only be lodged safely in the hands of the wise few. We hear the corruptions of the times attributed to universal suffrage. Yet these corruptions certainly are not peculiar to the United States: It is also said here, as it is in England, that our diffused and somewhat superficial education is merely unfitting the mass of men, who must be laborers, for any useful occupation.

This argument, reduced to plain terms, is simply this: that the mass of mankind are unfit to decide properly their own political and social condition; and that for the mass of mankind any but a very limited mental development is to be deprecated. It would be enough to say of this, that class government and popular ignorance have been tried for so many ages, and always with disaster and failure in the end, that I should think philanthropical historians would be tired of recommending them. But there is more to be said.

I feel that as a resident on earth, part owner of it for a time, unavoidably a member of society, I have a right to a voice in determining what my condition and what my chance in life shall be. I may be ignorant, I should be a very poor ruler of other people, but I am better capable of deciding some things that touch me nearly than another is. By what logic can I say that I should have a part in the conduct of this world and that my neighbor should not? Who is to decide what degree of intelligence shall fit a man for a share in the government? How are we to select the few capable men that are to rule all the rest? As a matter of fact, men have been rulers who had neither the average intelligence nor virtue of the people they governed. And, as a matter of historical experience, a class in power has always sought its own benefit rather than that of the whole people. Lunacy, extraordinary stupidity, and crime aside, a man is the best guardian of his own liberty and rights.

The English critics, who say we have taken the government from the capable few and given it to the people, speak of universal suffrage as a quack panacea of this "era of progress." But it is not the manufactured panacea of any theorist or philosopher whatever. It is the natural result of a diffused knowledge of human rights and of increasing intelligence. It is nothing against it that Napoleon III. used a mockery of it to govern France. It is not a device of the closet, but a method of government, which has naturally suggested itself to men as they have grown into a feeling of self-reliance and a consciousness that they have some right in the decision of their own destiny in the world. It is true that suffrage peculiarly fits a people virtuous and intelligent. But there has not yet been invented any government in which a people would thrive who were ignorant and vicious.

Our foreign critics seem to regard our "American system," by the way, as a sort of invention or patent right, upon which we are experimenting; forgetting that it is as legitimate a growth out of our circumstances as the English system is out of its antecedents. Our system is not the product of theorists or closet philosophers; but it was ordained in substance and inevitable from the day the first "town meeting" assembled in New England, and it was not in the power of Hamilton or any one else to make it otherwise.

So you must have education, now you have the ballot, say the critics of this era of progress; and this is another of your cheap inventions. Not that we undervalue book knowledge. Oh, no! but it really seems to us that a good trade, with the Lord's Prayer and the Ten Commandments back of it, would be the best thing for most of you. You must work for a living anyway; and why, now, should you unsettle your minds?

This is such an astounding view of human life and destiny that I do not know what to say to it. Did it occur to Mr. Froude to ask the man whether he would be contented with a good trade and the Ten Commandments? Perhaps the man would like eleven commandments? And, if he gets hold of the eleventh, he may want to know something more about his fellow-men, a little geography maybe, and some of Mr. Froude's history, and thus he may be led off into literature, and the Lord knows where.

The inference is that education—book fashion—will unfit the man for useful work. Mr. Froude here again stops at a half-truth. As a general thing, intelligence is useful in any position a man occupies. But it is true that there is a superficial and misdirected sort of education, so called, which makes the man who receives it despise labor; and it is also true that in the present educational revival there has been a neglect of training in the direction of skilled labor, and we all suffer more or less from cheap and dishonest work. But the way out of this, again, is forward, and not backward. It is a good sign, and not a stigma upon this era of progress, that people desire education. But this education must be of the whole man; he must be taught to work as well as to read, and he is, indeed, poorly educated if he is not fitted to do his work in the world. We certainly shall not have better workmen by having ignorant workmen. I need not say that the real education is that which will best fit a man for performing well his duties in life. If Mr. Froude, instead of his plaint over the scarcity of good mechanics, and of the Ten Commandments in England, had recommended the establishment of industrial schools, he would have spoken more to the purpose.

I should say that the fashionable skepticism of today, here and in England, is in regard to universal suffrage and the capacity of the people to govern themselves. The whole system is the sharp invention of Thomas Jefferson and others, by which crafty demagogues can rule. Instead of being, as we have patriotically supposed, a real progress in human development, it is only a fetich, which is becoming rapidly a failure. Now, there is a great deal of truth in the assertion that, whatever the form of government, the ablest men, or the strongest, or the most cunning in the nation, will rule. And yet it is true that in a popular government, like this, the humblest citizen, if he is wronged or oppressed, has in his hands a readier instrument of redress than he has ever had in any form of government. And it must not be forgotten that the ballot in the hands of all is perhaps the only safeguard against the tyranny of wealth in the hands of the few. It is true that bad men can band together and be destructive; but so they can in any government. Revolution by ballot is much safer than revolution by violence; and, granting that human nature is selfish, when the whole people are the government selfishness is on the side of the government. Can you mention any class in this country whose interest it is to overturn the government? And, then, as to the wisdom of the popular decisions by the ballot in this country. Look carefully at all the Presidential elections from Washington's down, and say, in the light of history, if the popular decision has not, every time, been the best for the country. It may not have seemed so to some of us at the time, but I think it is true, and a very significant fact.

Of course, in this affirmation of belief that one hundred years of popular government in this country is a real progress for humanity, and not merely a change from the rule of the fit to the rule of the cunning, we cannot forget that men are pretty much everywhere the same, and that we have abundant reason for national humility. We are pretty well aware that ours is not an ideal state of society, and should be so, even if the English who pass by did not revile us, wagging their heads. We might differ with them about the causes of our disorders. Doubtless, extended suffrage has produced certain results. It seems, strangely enough, to have escaped the observation of our English friends that to suffrage was due the late horse disease. No one can discover any other cause for it. But there is a cause for the various phenomena of this period of shoddy, of inflated speculation, of disturbance of all values, social, moral, political, and material, quite sufficient in the light of history to account for them. It is not suffrage; it is an irredeemable paper currency. It has borne its usual fruit with us, and neither foreign nor home critics can shift the responsibility of it upon our system of government. Yes, it is true, we have contrived to fill the world with our scandals of late. I might refer to a loose commercial and political morality; to betrayals of popular trust in politics; to corruptions in legislatures and in corporations; to an abuse of power in the public press, which has hardly yet got itself adjusted to its sudden accession of enormous influence. We complain of its injustice to individuals sometimes. We might imagine that something like this would occur.

A newspaper one day says: "We are exceedingly pained to hear that the Hon. Mr. Blank, who is running for Congress in the First District, has permitted his aged grandmother to go to the town poorhouse. What renders this conduct inexplicable is the fact that Mr. Blank is a man of large fortune."

The next day the newspaper says: "The Hon. Mr. Blank has not seen fit to deny the damaging accusation in regard to the treatment of his grandmother."

The next day the newspaper says: "Mr. Blank is still silent. He is probably aware that he cannot afford to rest under this grave charge."

The next day the newspaper asks: "Where's Blank? Has he fled?"

At last, goaded by these remarks, and most unfortunately for himself, Mr. Blank writes to the newspaper and most indignantly denies the charge; he never sent his grandmother to the poorhouse.

Thereupon the newspaper says: "Of course a rich man who would put his own grandmother in the poorhouse would deny it. Our informant was a gentleman of character. Mr. Blank rests the matter on his unsupported word. It is a question of veracity."

Or, perhaps, Mr. Blank, more unfortunately for himself, begins by making an affidavit, wherein he swears that he never sent his grandmother to the poorhouse, and that, in point of fact, he has not any grandmother whatever.

The newspaper then, in language that is now classical, "goes for" Mr. Blank. It says: "Mr. Blank resorts to the common device of the rogue —the affidavit. If he had been conscious of rectitude, would he not have relied upon his simple denial?"

Now, if an extreme case like this could occur, it would be bad enough. But, in our free society, the remedy would be at hand. The constituents of Mr. Blank would elect him in triumph. The newspaper would lose public confidence and support and learn to use its position more justly. What I mean to indicate by such an extreme instance as this is, that in our very license of individual freedom there is finally a correcting power.

We might pursue this general subject of progress by a comparison of the society of this country now with that of fifty years ago. I have no doubt that in every essential this is better than that, in manners, in morality, in charity and toleration, in education and religion. I know the standard of morality is higher. I know the churches are purer. Not fifty years ago, in a New England town, a distinguished doctor of divinity, the pastor of a leading church, was part owner in a distillery. He was a great light in his denomination, but he was an extravagant liver, and, being unable to pay his debts, he was arrested and put into jail, with the liberty of the "limits." In order not to interrupt his ministerial work, the jail limits were made to include his house and his church, so that he could still go in and out before his people. I do not think that could occur anywhere in the United States today.

I will close these fragmentary suggestions by saying that I, for one, should like to see this country a century from now. Those who live then will doubtless say of this period that it was crude, and rather disorderly, and fermenting with a great many new projects; but I have great faith that they will also say that the present extending notion, that the best government is for the people, by the people, was in the line of sound progress. I should expect to find faith in humanity greater and not less than it is now, and I should not expect to find that Mr. Froude's mournful expectation had been realized, and that the belief in a life beyond the grave had been withdrawn.

9 789357 945684